Last . . . and least.

As usual, gym class began with "choosing teams."

Bob Cheatham was the captain of the red team. "I choose Tom Ballan!" he said importantly.

Big surprise, *thought Marty.*

"I choose Tipper Grant," the blue team captain called out.

Tipper had lots of friends.

Marty's shoulders sagged. He looked down at a crack on the gym floor. One by one the children were chosen.

Marty tried to think about something else. He could only think about the teams. A silent prayer kept calling in his head. Pick me. Pick me.

"Distinguished by Duffey's skill in making Marty's inner feelings ring true." —*Kirkus Reviews*

THE MATH WIZ

BY BETSY DUFFEY

Illustrated by Janet Wilson

SCHOLASTIC INC.
New York Toronto London Auckland Sydney

ISBN 0-590-66649-5

Text copyright © 1990 by Betsy Duffey.
Illustrations copyright © 1990 by Janet Wilson.
All rights reserved. Published by Scholastic Inc.,
555 Broadway, New York, NY 10012, by arrangement with Penguin
Books USA Inc. SCHOLASTIC and associated logos are trademarks
and/or registered trademarks of Scholastic Inc.

12 11 10 9 8 7 6 5 4 3 2   12   0 1 2/0

Printed in the U.S.A.   40

For my mother

CONTENTS

THE P.E. PROBLEM

Marty Malone was a Math Wizard. He could add, subtract, multiply, and divide better than any other third grader at Danville School.

When he was only four years old he did his first subtraction problem. He was sitting on the floor with his baby brother, Tad. Baby Tad was sucking hard on his bottle. His chubby hands held the bottle tightly. His eyes were almost closed.

Even way back then Marty liked to think of

everything as a math problem. He watched the baby for a while. Then he thought:

BABY + BOTTLE = QUIET BABY

Then he started wondering:

BABY − BOTTLE = ???????????

What??

Marty always said that every problem needs an answer.

So he reached over and pulled the bottle away from Baby Tad. It wasn't easy. The bottle was tight in Tad's mouth. Marty pulled with all his strength, harder, harder . . . *Pop!* The bottle popped out of the baby's mouth.

BABY − BOTTLE = ?????????????

For a few seconds there was no reaction. Then Baby Tad's eyes blinked open. His face began to wrinkle. It wrinkled more and more. Then—

Waaaaaaaaaaaaaaaaaaaa!!!!!!!!!

BABY − BOTTLE = WAAAAAAAAAAAA!!!

"What are you doing in there?" called his mother from the kitchen.

"Math, Mom," Marty answered, "just math."

Quickly he stuck the bottle back into the baby's mouth.

All was quiet again.

By the time he started kindergarten he already knew how to add and subtract, to carry and borrow numbers.

The summer after kindergarten he did his first multiplication problem.

He had only had his guinea pigs, Plus and Minus, for a month when it started. Plus had four babies.

Everyone was delighted.

His mom brought them fresh lettuce every day from the store. His dad brought home extra newspapers from the office to put in the bottom of the cages.

Tad, who was now no longer a baby, loved to hear them squeak. Every time the refrigerator door opened the guinea pigs thought it was dinnertime and they would start squeaking. Tad was always opening the door just to hear them.

One month later, those baby guinea pigs were grown and THEY had babies! Then another month passed and THEIR babies were grown and had babies.

Marty was thrilled. He made a chart for his bedroom wall that looked like this:

$1 \times 4 = 4$

$2 \times 4 = 8$

$4 \times 4 = 16$

By the end of the summer he had 30 guinea pigs!

Everyone else was not thrilled.

His mother got tired of buying all that lettuce. Thirty guinea pigs eat a lot of lettuce.

His dad got tired of bringing home newspapers.

Everyone got tired of the *squeak, squeak, squeak*.

The multiplication problem stopped when Marty's mom called the pet shop to come pick up all the guinea pigs. Only Minus got to stay.

Marty's mom made a new family rule:

THE PEOPLE IN THIS FAMILY MUST
ALWAYS OUTNUMBER THE PETS

She wrote it on a piece of paper and put it up on the refrigerator with a magnet.

At the bottom of the paper Marty wrote:

PEOPLE > PETS

Marty always thought that there was no problem too big or too long for him to solve.

He had a poster taped over his desk in his bedroom. He made it himself with poster board and markers. It said:

MATH WIZ AT WORK

NO PROBLEM TOO BIG

NO PROBLEM TOO LONG

But now Marty had a problem that seemed too big for him to solve. A problem that was making his life miserable.

He called it the P.E. Problem. He thought of it like this:

MATH WIZ + P.E. = MISERY

PICK ME!!!

Marty had only been at Danville School for two weeks. Two weeks doesn't seem like a very long time if you are at the beach or on winter vacation, but the first two weeks at a new school can seem like a long, long time. It did to Marty.

It was long enough for Marty to find out two things that would cause his P.E. Problem. The first was that all third graders had to take gym class, called P.E. at Danville School. The second thing was that Marty Malone was the worst kid in the class.

Being good at math did not prepare you for everything in the world. Being good at math did not prepare you for P.E.

Marty sat at the desk in his bedroom. He closed the door so that Tad would not come in and bother him.

Tad loved to sneak into his room and break his pencils. He would take them one by one and press the point down hard on the table until, *crack*, the pencil would break. Then he would laugh.

Marty did not think it was at all funny.

He was supposed to be doing his homework but he kept thinking about his problem, the P.E. Problem.

What made P.E. such a problem?

He looked around his room. Anyone could look at this room and tell that Marty did not like sports. There were no golden soccer or basketball trophies on his shelves. There were no baseball pennants tacked up on his walls. No balls, mitts, or rackets were scattered across his floor.

So, Marty didn't like sports.

That had never been a problem at Marty's old school. He had liked gym class at his old school just fine. You didn't have to like sports or even be good at sports to have fun playing games with the other kids. Sports were fun at his old school.

Things were different at Danville School. Coach McMillian, the P.E. teacher at Danville School, had different ideas about sports. To Coach, sports were not games for having fun, sports were serious business.

Worst of all was something that Coach McMillian called:

"CHOOSING TEAMS."

At the beginning of each class Coach picked two captains. He went down a list of the class alphabetically. Each day the next two kids on the list would be the Captains of the Day.

All the kids would line up on a black line on the gym floor, and the captains would take turns picking out the kids they wanted to have on their teams.

First one captain would choose a kid, then the other captain would choose, until all the kids were chosen.

The kids who were good at sports were always chosen first. The kids who had lots of friends were always chosen next.

Every day for two weeks Marty had been chosen last.

Being chosen last at P.E. was the worst thing about Danville School.

Marty put his head down on his desk. He remembered P.E. class that morning. It still hurt his feelings to think about it.

As usual, the class began with "choosing teams."

Bob Cheatham was the captain of the red team. "I choose Tom Ballan!" he said importantly.

Big surprise, thought Marty. Tom Ballan was great at sports.

"I choose Tipper Grant," the blue team captain called out.

Tipper had lots of friends.

Marty's shoulders sagged. He looked down at a crack on the gym floor.

One by one the children were chosen. As their names were called they ran forward excitedly to the red or the blue team.

When they got to their team they clapped hands in a high five with the other players.

"All right!!!!" they yelled as they clapped.

As the children were chosen Marty tried to think about something else. He practiced addition in his head.

$2+2 = 4 \ldots 4+4 = 8$.

It didn't work.

He could only think about the teams. A silent prayer kept calling in his head. *Pick me. Pick me.*

"Susie Bartow," the red team captain called.

$8+8 = 16 \ldots$ *Pick me. Pick me,* his brain said.

"Randy Sims."

Pick me. Pick me.

"Julie Jackson."

Pick meeeeeeee!!!!

Slowly the picking went on and on. Still Marty

stood on the line. Finally only two kids were left.

Marty looked up from the floor to sneak a peek at the other kid—Billy Beason.

Billy was in the highest math group with Marty. But in P.E.—well, in P.E. Billy missed the ball when he batted at softball and stumbled when he tried to run fast.

Billy was probably the second worst kid in P.E. Before Marty had started school two weeks ago Billy had probably been the WORST kid in P.E.

Billy was looking down at his shoes, too. He was used to being chosen last.

"Billy Beason," Bob called. He rolled his eyes up to the ceiling.

Billy began walking slowly toward the red team. The teams were already lining up at the volleyball net. Marty noticed that no one held up their hand for Billy to clap.

Being good at math didn't get you far in P.E., Marty had thought as he headed for the blue team.

★   ★   ★

Crack!

Uh-oh! Tad was at the pencils again. Marty jumped up from his desk and grabbed his pencil box. He pushed Tad out of the room. He had work to do. He closed the door and locked it this time.

He took out a blank sheet of notebook paper and put it on his desk.

The fresh white paper gave him hope.

He looked up at the sign over his desk.

NO PROBLEM TOO BIG

He could figure this one out!

At the top of the paper he wrote:

THE P.E. PROBLEM

Then he wrote:

MATH WIZ + P.E. = MISERY

He chewed on the eraser of his pencil for a minute as he looked at the paper. Then he wrote:

MATH WIZ − P.E. = ???????

He had to get out of P.E.

But how?

He drew a circle around the letters *P.E.*
Under it he wrote:

HOW TO GET OUT OF P.E.

He chewed on his eraser some more.
Suddenly he had a plan.
A plan that would get him out of P.E.
In big black letters he wrote two words:

ACE BANDAGE

Then for the first time in two weeks he
smiled.

THE ACE BANDAGE PLAN

B*eep* . . . *Beep* . . . *Beep* . . . *Beep* . . .

It was morning.

Marty reached over without getting out of bed and pushed the black button on top of his alarm clock. The beeping stopped.

He rested his head back on the pillow without opening his eyes. For a moment he imagined that he was back in his old bedroom before the move.

"Marty. . . . Marty!"

He imagined that he could hear his best friend from his old school, Jimmy, calling him to come outside and play.

"Marty! . . . Marty! Get up, Marty!"

It wasn't Jimmy. It was his mother! He pulled the covers over his head. She had ruined his daydream.

"Marty, get up for school!"

School!

Marty had almost forgotten his plan. He reached under his pillow and found the folded piece of notebook paper. He brought it out from under his pillow and sat up.

He held it tightly in his hand for a moment and then unfolded it.

He knew exactly what it said. But it gave him courage to see it again in writing.

HOW TO GET OUT OF P.E.
ACE BANDAGE

Marty got dressed in a hurry. He made his bed, brushed his teeth, and gathered up his homework and put it into his backpack. Then he made his move.

He ran into his parents' room and opened his father's sock drawer.

There it was, the Ace bandage.

His dad had sprained his ankle once on a hiking trip. Marty's mom had bought the Ace bandage for him at a drugstore.

Marty remembered how he had put it on. The bandage was a long, brown, stretchy piece of cloth. His dad had wrapped it around and around his ankle—about 20 times. Then he had fastened it with two special clips to keep it from coming undone. It had been smooth and tight on his leg.

Marty poked the Ace bandage box into his backpack and headed downstairs.

Mission accomplished!

If he put the bandage on his leg then everyone would think that he had a sprained leg and he would not have to go to P.E.

He could just imagine it:

Marty would come limping into the gym.

All the kids would drop their balls and rackets and come running over to him.

Slowly he would roll up the leg of his jeans

and the Ace bandage would be wrapped tightly and smoothly around his leg.

"Oooooooooooooooooooo!" they would say together.

Coach would come hurrying over, filled with concern.

"Here, son," he would say, "lean on me. Come and sit down. No need for you to take P.E. today."

"It's nothing," Marty would say, waving them away.

"It's . . ."

"Marty!" his mom called again from the kitchen. "Come on down. You don't want to be late for school, do you?"

"No, Mom. I don't want to be late for school!" Marty answered as he ran down the stairs. And for once it was true.

CHUBBY BUBBY BIG WAD GUM

When Marty got to school he went straight to the boys' bathroom. No one else was there. Everyone else was hurrying to class. The last bell was about to ring. He didn't have much time.

He took the bandage out of the box and unwound it. It was a lot longer than he had remembered.

He pulled up the leg of his jeans and tried to wind the bandage around his leg. It kept getting tangled. Finally he got it on.

It didn't look as smooth and tight as it had on his father's ankle. It looked bumpy and loose.

He looked in the box for the special clips. It was empty.

NO CLIPS!

He turned it over and shook it. He felt in every corner of the box. There were no clips in the box.

Marty didn't know quite what to do. He had gotten this far. He didn't want to give up now.

He checked his pocket—two nickels, one rock, one pencil stub, and one stick of Chubby Bubby Big Wad Gum.

He picked out the gum.

Perfect!

He put the piece of gum into his mouth and began to chew it. When it was nice and soft he stuck it on the end of the bandage. Then he stuck the end of the bandage down with the gum.

Marty patted the bandage a few times to try to smooth it out.

He frowned. It did not feel very tight.

He stopped and thought for a second.

Maybe he should put the bandage back and forget the whole plan.

Brinnnngggg!

The last bell!

No time left to change his mind. The bandage would have to do.

Carefully, he pulled the leg of his jeans back down over the bandage and hurried on to class.

Marty stayed in his seat all morning. He was afraid if he moved his leg the bandage would come undone.

He could feel it slip a little every time he moved.

He didn't go to the water fountain. He didn't go to the boys' bathroom at break time. He didn't even go to the pencil sharpener once.

Finally the bell rang for P.E. Marty made his way down the hall. He tried to walk with his leg stiff.

Step . . . Thump . . . Step . . . Thump.

He kept looking down to check the bandage. It was already down around his foot like a sock. It didn't feel at all tight.

It was so loose that Marty could not feel it at all. It sure wouldn't convince Coach McMillian if it got any lower.

Step . . . Thump . . . Step . . . Thump.

He looked down the hall. He was almost to the gym. Just a little farther.

Step . . . Thump. Almost there.

He glanced down to check the bandage again.

Marty stopped and stared down at his leg. He didn't want to believe what he saw.

There was a long brown tail coming out from the bottom of his jeans. On the end of the tail was the giant wad of Chubby Bubby Big Wad Gum!

What should he do?

Should he stop and try to pick up the bandage or try to make it to the gym? If he could get to the gym maybe he could fix it before anyone noticed.

He decided to keep on walking. He didn't have far to go. He hoped no one would step on the gum.

Step . . . Thump . . . Step . . . Thump.

He walked a little faster.

He looked down the hall to see how much farther he had to go.

Uh-oh! Down the hall, coming right toward him, was Mr. Hardeman, the principal. Mr. Hardeman was looking right at him.

He tried to make his face look as normal as possible. He tried to walk as normally as possible. He tried not to look like a boy with a long brown tail coming out of his jeans leg.

Mr. Hardeman was a strict principal. He would not think it was very funny.

As Marty watched, Mr. Hardeman came closer . . . closer . . . closer . . .

Mr. Hardeman nodded as he passed Marty without looking down.

Whewwwww!

He didn't notice the bandage!

Marty sighed with relief. All clear!

He stopped for a few seconds and leaned back against the lockers in the hall to catch his breath.

He had made it past Mr. Hardeman. Now he was almost to the gym door.

He stopped and looked down one more time to check his bandage.

At the bottom of his pants leg he could see his bare ankle. He looked closer.

Double Uh-oh! No bandage!

He pulled up his pants leg and looked one more time. He stared at his bare leg. The bandage was gone.

Marty felt sick. He decided that he better find the bandage and pick it up before someone stepped on the gum.

He turned around and looked down the hall to find it.

No bandage.

Where did it go?

Marty saw something moving on the floor at the end of the hall.

Something long and brown.

Triple Uh-oh!

The long brown something was following along behind Mr. Hardeman.

He could no longer see the Chubby Bubby Big Wad Gum. It was stuck to the bottom of Mr. Hardeman's shoe!

Mr. Hardeman must have stepped on the gum. The Ace bandage was still stuck to the gum, trailing behind the principal like a long tail.

He could see the other kids in the hall turning to look at Mr. Hardeman as he passed them. Some of them giggled.

Mr. Hardeman nodded to each kid as he passed.

Marty shook his head. Boy, would he be mad later when he saw what had been following him. Boy, would he be mad at Marty if he found out who did it.

Marty felt even sicker.

He did not look back again.

Before he went into the gym he pulled his piece of notebook paper out of his pocket and drew a dark black line through the words:

ACE BANDAGE

Then he started into the gym for P.E.

His plan had failed.

He was not going to get out of P.E. today.

CAPTAINS OF THE DAY

Tweeeeeeeeet!! Coach McMillian blew his whistle.

Marty stopped at the door to the gym. He still felt sick. His stomach hurt and his palms were cold and sweaty.

The other kids pushed past him as if he were invisible.

He had seen a movie once about an invisible man. In the movie the man could do wonderful things because people could not see him. He surprised bank robbers at a holdup. He listened in unseen on the plans of gangsters and stopped their crimes.

After the movie Marty thought about how much fun it would be to be invisible. Now, after two weeks of feeling invisible at Danville School he realized how wrong he was.

He smoothed down his T-shirt and put his hands in his pockets. He had worn his favorite T-shirt today to give him courage.

It was bright blue covered with white numbers. The numbers made a long problem. The problem started at the front of the shirt—2,345 + 4,563 − 3,678 + 9,561 − 2,890. . . . The numbers went on and on all over the shirt. At the bottom of the back of the shirt was an = sign but no answer.

One night Marty had worked the problem. It had taken him two hours to figure it out. 3,742 was the answer. Only a Math Wiz could do a problem like that!

"Move *it!* Move *it!*" Coach called out to the kids.

Coach used to be in the army. He still acted

like a drill sergeant. He rocked back and forth on his heels and tried to suck in his stomach.

The kids began to line up on the long black line that ran down the side of the basketball court.

P.E. was serious business.

Kate Ellen Johnson pushed Marty with her elbow as she passed by. Kate Ellen was always in a hurry. When she walked she moved her arms back and forth as if she was pushing people out of the way.

Sally Long followed her like a shadow.

"Coach, Coach McMillian," Kate Ellen called out in a high, squeaky voice.

"Coach, isn't it our turn to be Captains of the Day? See, we're up to the *J*s. Johnson should be next."

Coach gave her a tired look and rocked back and forth on his heels some more.

Kate Ellen wrinkled her nose up as if she smelled something awful. She was always doing that. Marty hated it. It always made him feel like the something awful was him.

"See, we were up to Jenkins yesterday. Now we should be up to Johnson."

Coach gave Kate Ellen a long, hard look.

"And then comes *L* for Long," said Sally like an echo.

"Move *it*, girls," said Coach loudly. "Line up now or there won't be any teams today—there will be LAPS to run."

Kate Ellen and Sally hurried toward the black line.

Coach turned to face the other kids. Some were not yet lined up.

"I SAID there will be LAPS to run," he said in a loud voice. "Would anyone like to run some LAPS today?"

At the sound of the word *laps* the class began to line up quickly. Nobody liked to run laps. Marty hurried over to his place on the line.

Why would anyone WANT to be Captain of the Day, Marty wondered. He could think of nothing worse than standing up in front of the class picking out the kids to be on his team.

He could just imagine it.

The kids would be lined up on the black line.

Coach would call out, "Captain of the Day, MARTY MALONE."

Marty would step forward from the black line and would call out his first choice.

"Tom Ballan," he would say.

"No, thanks!" Tom Ballan would say and he would head toward the other team.

"Tipper Grant," Marty would say.

"No, thanks!" Tipper would say and she would go to the other team, too.

Pretty soon all the kids in the class would be on the other team.

It would be like one long subtraction problem. One by one each kid would be subtracted until there was only Marty left.

He would be left alone on the blue team.

Being Captain of the Day might even be worse than being chosen last.

If they were up to the Ls, then the Ms were next. Malone started with M. Tomorrow would be Marty's turn to be Captain of the Day.

He decided to be absent tomorrow.

Tweeeeeeet!

Uh-oh! P.E. was starting.

"Volleyball! Choose teams!" called Coach.

Double Uh-oh! Marty hated volleyball.

"Captains of the Day . . . Kate Ellen Johnson and Sally Long."

Triple Uh-oh! thought Marty.

He settled in to be chosen last.

The teams were chosen. Last again!

Marty decided that today he would try as hard as he could. Today he would be good at P.E.

The teams lined up and faced each other at the volleyball net. They took turns bouncing the ball back and forth over the net.

Coach blew his whistle and the game began. Everyone was serious now. The ball went back and forth across the net and the kids tried hard not to miss it when it came to them.

Marty watched the ball closely. If it came to him he would be ready.

Finally the ball came high over the net right toward Marty. His big chance. His chance to get noticed.

"Get it, Marty!" someone called. They were cheering for him!

"Go, Marty!" He wouldn't let them down. This time he would hit the ball back over the net.

The ball seemed like it moved in slow motion as it made its way down.

Marty reached up his hands . . .

Kerthump!!

The ball hit Marty right on the top of his head.

Marty looked at his hands in disbelief. How could they have failed him?

Coach groaned. The other team made a point.

Marty felt his face turn red. He moved to the back of the volleyball court. He was no longer interested in the game.

It was hopeless.

He kept his eyes on the floor and hoped that the ball would not come to him again.

When he looked up he could see Billy Beason on the other team staring at him.

He must think I'm a real nerd, thought Marty.

He wished P.E. would be over. He looked up at the clock on the wall of the gym. In fifteen minutes he would be in Miss Williams's math class.

Miss Williams was the one good thing about Danville School. Her class was wonderful.

It had problems, problems, and more problems. And Marty was an expert at solving problems.

What was the solution to the P.E. Problem? Marty wondered.

MATH WIZ + P.E. = MISERY

There had to be a way to make that problem come out differently.

Somehow, some way, today during math class he would solve the P.E. Problem.

But first he had to make it through P.E.

BOY + GOOD AT MATH = ????

Tweeeeeeeet!

"Take five!" yelled Coach.

That was Coach's way of saying, "Take a water break."

Some of the kids went to the water fountain. Some of the kids sat down on the bleachers and talked to each other.

Marty did not go with them. He was left alone.

At the other end of the gym Marty could see

Tom Ballan. He stood out from the other kids, bouncing the volleyball on his knee. First one knee—then the other—then up to his head—then knee, elbow, head.

Wow. He was terrific.

If Marty was the worst kid in P.E., Tom Ballan was the best.

He was tall and was the only kid in the class with muscles. He wore his T-shirt sleeves rolled up to the shoulders and was always stretching. Now he stretched out his arm and flexed it up. As he flexed his arm a real muscle bumped up.

Marty looked down at his own arm. He did not bend it up and flex it. He knew there would be no bump on his arm.

Boys with muscles were good at sports. Tom Ballan was always chosen first for volleyball and dodgeball teams.

Marty thought of it like a math problem.

BOY + MUSCLES = GOOD AT SPORTS

He thought of it another way:

BOY + GOOD AT SPORTS = ???

What?
FRIENDS, he decided.

BOY + GOOD AT SPORTS = FRIENDS

What was so neat about sports anyway?

Why couldn't something HE was good at be considered neat—like math?

Marty sighed. He tried to make it into a problem:

BOY + GOOD AT MATH = ????

He couldn't finish the problem.

He didn't think the answer was FRIENDS. But what was it??? He tried again.

BOY + GOOD AT MATH = A'S ON REPORT CARD

A's on report cards sure were nice but right now he sure would like the answer to be *friends*, too.

If you can throw a ball or run fast, crowds of people cheer and go wild over you. You just didn't see crowds of people going wild over math, did you?

But . . . what if they did????

He could just imagine it.

The gym would be filled with hundreds of cheering kids. In front of a large blackboard would be Marty, his blue uniform shiny under the bright lights. Beside him in a red uniform, the challenger.

The cheerleaders would be twirling around swishing their pom-poms. The pep band would be playing and the kids in the bleachers would clap along in time to the music.

Tweeet! Coach would blow his whistle and Marty and the challenger would begin to add long columns of numbers.

"Go, Marty!" someone would call out just like they had in the volleyball game. But this time would not be like the volleyball game. This time he could do it.

The kids would cheer him on as he added the long columns of numbers.

"MATH WIZ!!!!!"

"MATH WIZ!!!!!!"

"MATH . . ."

Tweeeeeeeet!

Coach's whistle interrupted his daydream.

"That's it for today! Move on out!"

P.E. was over.

Marty began to move toward the door with the other kids.

He had survived another day of P.E.

"Move it! Move it," Coach called out, louder this time. "I SAID, move on out!"

"With pleasure!" Marty said softly to himself and he headed out the gym door to math class.

TRIPLE UH-OH

The kids in the third grade divided up for math. The kids who were the best at math went to Miss Williams's room. The other kids went to different rooms.

Marty took a seat in the back row and began to organize his pencils. He had three pencils— all with sharp points. If one broke, he would always have a spare.

Miss Williams was passing out white sheets of paper. She placed the papers face down on the children's desks.

"We'll start the class with a time test," she announced. "Subtraction."

"Oh, no!" Marty heard someone whisper.

Marty smiled. He loved time tests. What could be more fun than a whole page of problems just waiting to be solved?

Miss Williams finished handing out the tests. She reached in her desk and pulled out a small silver stopwatch.

"You will have ten minutes." She held up the watch.

"Ready. . . . BEGIN!" she called out as she pushed the button on the top of the stopwatch.

Quickly the children turned over their papers and began to work the problems. If they finished all the problems before the ten minutes was over, they raised their hands.

Marty finished all his problems in only four minutes. His hand shot up.

Miss Williams hurried over to his desk.

"Very good, Marty," she whispered as she wrote *4 min. 20 sec.* on the bottom of his paper.

She smiled at him.

"You may work in your workbook until the others finish."

Marty looked around the room. No one else was finished. Marty had five more minutes to wait before the test would be over.

He took out his workbook. He opened it but he did not work in it. Instead he pulled his piece of notebook paper out of his pocket, the P.E. Problem. He put it inside his workbook so it would look like he was working in his workbook.

He looked at the problem:

MATH WIZ + P.E. = MISERY

He chewed on the eraser of his pencil for a few seconds as he looked at the paper. Then he wrote:

CHANGE THE PROBLEM!!

Last week in math class they learned that if you change any part of a problem, the answer changes, too. In the P.E. Problem the answer was misery. Marty really wanted to change that answer. But what could he change in the problem?

He looked at the first part—MATH WIZ. Math Wiz was Marty. He was good in math. He had tried as hard as he could to be good at volleyball. He just was not good in P.E. He really couldn't change that.

He wrote beside MATH WIZ: CAN'T CHANGE THIS and drew a line to where the problem said MATH WIZ.

He looked at the next part—P.E. Marty had already tried to get out of P.E. All third graders had to take P.E. He shook his head and wrote: CAN'T CHANGE THIS and drew a line to P.E.

He chewed on his eraser some more.

"Marty. . . . Marty Malone. . . ."

Uh-oh! Back to math class.

"Did you hear me, Marty?"

Double Uh-oh! Miss Williams did not look happy.

"Uh, yes," said Marty.

"Then could you please give us the next answer?"

"Answer??" Marty said. They were checking the answers on the time test. He did not even know what problem they were on.

He looked down at his test paper, helplessly.

"Go ahead, Marty," Miss Williams said. "We're waiting."

Miss Williams did not sound pleased. She tapped her foot.

Tap . . . Tap . . . Tap . . .

Marty did not look up from his paper.

The class was silent. The only sound was the sound of Miss Williams's foot.

Tap . . . Tap . . . Tap . . .

"I know, Miss Williams!" a high, squeaky voice called out.

It was Kate Ellen, waving her hand wildly in the air. "I know, it's 68!"

"Kate Ellen!" Miss Williams said, turning to the other side of the room. "We do not answer out of turn!"

"Sorry," she said, sounding not one bit sorry.

Kate Ellen looked directly at Marty and wrinkled her nose and smiled.

She had saved him!

Marty began to like the way she wrinkled her nose.

He quickly shuffled his P.E. Problem under his test so that Miss Williams would not see it.

He looked down at his test and looked for the answer that was 68. Now he knew right where they were checking.

He hoped that Miss Williams would call on him again.

He raised his hand but she did not give him a second chance.

"Tom Ballan, could you give us the answer to the last problem?"

There was a long silence.

"234?" Tom answered.

"The correct answer is 334," Miss Williams said.

Someone giggled. Tom looked down at his paper and turned red.

Tom looked like he felt as bad as Marty had felt when he missed the volleyball in P.E.

Miss Williams began to collect the papers.

"You may work in your workbooks until the bell rings. Work the page numbers written on the board," she said as she walked down each row of desks picking up the test papers.

When she got to Marty's desk she reached down and picked up his test paper.

This time she did not smile.

Marty looked down at the spot where his test paper had been. The P.E. Problem had been under the test paper.

BOTH were gone.

Triple Uh-oh!

Miss Williams had the P.E. Problem!

A NOTE TO MARTY

Marty worked a few problems in his workbook. He tried to concentrate on his work but he couldn't.

He looked around the room.

Billy Beason was staring at him again.

He wondered why. He looked down to be sure his zipper was zipped. He licked his hand and smoothed down his cowlick.

Billy still stared.

He must think I'm a real nerd, Marty thought again.

Marty looked up to the front of the room where Miss Williams was correcting the math tests.

When she came to his she would know all about his P.E. Problem. Worse than that she would know about the Ace bandage.

By now he was sure the Mr. Hardeman had found out about the Ace bandage on his shoe. He would be looking for the kid who did that to him. He would be looking for Marty.

Miss Williams would probably send him to the principal's office.

He tried to work a few more problems.

Then he put his head down on his desk and closed his eyes.

"Psssst," someone hissed from the other side of the room.

"Pssssst!"

He looked up and saw a note being passed. He wondered who the note was for.

The class was good at note passing.

Kate Ellen had the note. She pretended to yawn. When she stretched out her arm she dropped the note on Susie Bartow's desk.

Susie tapped the back of Julie Jackson's neck with the note. Julie reached back and scratched her neck and took the note.

Julie put the note in her shoe and lifted her foot up high beside Bob Cheatham's desk.

Bob took the note and pulled a large rubber band out of his pocket. He put the rubber band around the note and pulled it back like a slingshot. Then—*whooosh*—he shot the note directly onto Marty's desk.

Everyone giggled. Miss Williams looked up quickly from her desk.

"Class, is there a problem?" she asked.

"No, Miss Williams," someone answered.

"Then let's get on with our work," she said.

Marty waited a minute until Miss Williams looked back down at the papers on her desk. Then he looked at the note.

To: Marty was written on the front of the note.

Who could have sent him a note? he wondered.

He began to unfold the note.

Bbbrrrinnnnnggggg!!

The bell rang. School was over.

Miss Wiliams looked up from her desk.

Marty quickly stuck the note in his back pocket. He did not want to get into any MORE trouble with Miss Williams.

The note would have to wait.

3,742

The other kids picked up their books and headed toward the door.

Miss Williams stood at the door and handed back the time tests as each one left.

Marty stayed in his seat. He couldn't decide. Should he wait until everyone left and then go up and get his papers from Miss Williams? Or should he try to slip on through with them?

He watched as each kid got back their test. When they saw their grades some of them groaned. He watched Billy get his test back. Billy looked at his paper and smiled. Then Billy stopped just outside the door and looked back like he was waiting for someone.

Marty sighed. He wished that Billy was waiting for HIM but he knew it wasn't possible. Billy thought he was a nerd.

He decided not to go out until all the other kids were gone. He put his head down on his desk until he heard the last kid leave the room.

When he looked up Billy was gone.

Marty got up and moved slowly to the door.

Without saying a word, Miss Williams handed him his papers. He could tell by the way it felt that it was more than one paper. He could tell that it was more than two papers. It felt like about three papers.

Marty moved like a zombie through the door and headed slowly toward home.

He was afraid to look at the papers. He carried them tightly in his fist, slightly crumpled.

He decided that one of the papers must be a note to his parents. He could just imagine what it said.

Dear Mr. and Mrs. Malone,

Your son has been in a little trouble today. He attached an Ace bandage to the principal's shoe with a wad of Chubby Bubby Big Wad Gum.

It was true. He looked down at the sidewalk. The pavement blurred.

His parents would have to sign the note and send it back.

They would not be happy about this.

Usually when Marty got home from school he ran right into the kitchen for a snack. But today he wasn't at all hungry. Today he went straight upstairs to his room.

He put the papers on his desk and smoothed them out. He sat down.

Then he took a deep breath and looked down at the top paper.

It was his time test.

A + was written on the top line.

Miss Williams must not be too *mad*, thought Marty, *if she gave me an* A +. He began to feel a little better.

He moved the test paper to the side and stared down at the next page. It was the P.E. Problem, but something had been added to it.

Miss Williams had corrected it just like she corrected all his math papers!

Under the problem she had written in red ink:

Another way to change the answer to a problem is to add something new to the problem.

Then she wrote:

MATH WIZ + P.E. + A FRIEND = ??????

A friend?

A friend would make P.E. a lot better. Marty wished that adding a friend to his life was as easy as writing it down on a piece of notebook paper. It wasn't that easy!

He crumpled the paper into a ball and threw it into his wastebasket. The P.E. Problem had caused him enough trouble.

That left one more sheet of paper from Miss Williams. It was not a note to his parents.

It was blue and was printed with big block letters.

Marty read it. Then he smiled.

MATH CLUB PICNIC
WHEN: WEDNESDAY AFTER SCHOOL
WHERE: BALL FIELD
WHO: ALL MEMBERS AND ALL
STUDENTS WHO LIKE MATH
WHAT TO BRING: PAPER AND
PENCILS

At the the bottom of the page in red ink Miss Williams had written:

The perfect place for a Math Wiz to find a friend!

Marty sat at his desk and thought about the math club picnic. Lots of kids would be there—kids who liked math like Marty.

He decided he would go.

Suddenly Marty felt hungry. As he headed downstairs to the kitchen for his snack, he remembered his note.

He sat down on the bottom step and took it out of his pocket. He quickly unfolded it.

It was the shortest note that Marty had ever seen. It had no words at all, only a number.

3,742

He stared at the note for a few seconds. Then he remembered—

His T-shirt!

3,742 was the answer to the problem on his T-shirt! He turned the paper over.

From: Billy, it said on the back.

Billy Beason! That's why Billy had been staring at him all day. He was staring at the problem on Marty's T-shirt.

Maybe Billy didn't think he was a nerd.

Maybe Billy had been waiting for HIM outside the door after math class.

Marty wondered if Billy would be at the math club picnic.

Marty smiled again.

BOY + GOOD AT MATH = FRIENDS

Maybe it could be true after all.

THE SOLUTION

The next day Marty ran all the way to school. Today he would solve the P.E. Problem!

He hurried down the hall to class. Ahead he could see the door to Mr. Hardeman's office. He walked a little slower.

He remembered the Ace bandage. He remembered Mr. Hardeman walking down the hall with the Ace bandage attached to his shoe. He remembered the note to his parents that he had imagined yesterday.

Your son has been in a little trouble today . . .

Was he in trouble?

Was Mr. Hardeman looking for him?

What had happened to the Ace bandage?

As Marty passed the door to the principal's office, he began to tiptoe. He didn't want to run into Mr. Hardeman today.

Bang!

The door flew open.

Mr. Hardeman!!!! Marty froze.

"Good morning, Marty," Mr. Hardeman said. He nodded and hurried past Marty.

He didn't look at all mad!

He must not know!

Before the door could close again a hand reached out and put a trash can into the hall for the morning trash pickup.

Marty looked down at the pile of trash in the trash can and smiled. Right on top was something long and brown and stretchy—the Ace bandage.

Mr. Hardeman must not be looking for him if he was throwing away the evidence!

Marty started to pick up the Ace bandage,

then he changed his mind. He gave it one farewell glance and headed down the hall to class.

He wouldn't be needing it anymore.

Class began.

All morning Marty watched the clock.

The bell for P.E. rang and for the first time since he started Danville School the sound of the P.E. bell did not make Marty feel sick. He didn't mind going to P.E.

He hurried to the gym.

Tweeeeetttttt!

Today the sound of Coach's whistle didn't bother Marty.

"Dodgeball—choose teams," called Coach.

Today "choosing teams" didn't bother Marty.

"Captains of the Day . . . Sam Miller and Marty Malone."

Even being Captain of the Day didn't bother Marty.

He hurried forward from the black line to choose his team. He didn't feel at all invisible.

He looked down the line at the kids in his class: Kate Ellen, Tom, Billy, Sally, and all the others.

For the first time he saw them as different people, not just as a group.

Some were good in P.E., others good in art. Some were good in math, others in writing. Every one of them was different. Every one of them was strong in some ways and not so strong in other ways just like Marty.

Today he was glad that he was good in math. Math was what he liked. Math was what made him happy. So what if he was not good in P.E.? Everyone was not good at everything.

He stood tall and got ready to call out his first choice for the red team.

Tom Ballan and Tipper Grant leaned forward, ready to be called.

"I choose . . ." Marty said clearly and proudly . . .

"Billy Beason."

Billy looked up at Marty. His mouth dropped open in surprise. He had NEVER been chosen first in P.E.

His face broke into a big grin as he ran forward from the black line.

Smack!! went his hand against Marty's as they gave each other the high five. And together they broke into a yell—

"All right!!!!!!!"

MATH WIZ + P.E. + A FRIEND = ALL RIGHT!!!!!!!!